W9-CSR-379

...rical
...y. Other
... of the author's
...ts or places or

...t 10010
...shing USA
...right of reproduction in whole or

...k of Bonnier Publishing USA, and
...emark of Bonnier Publishing USA.
...ging-in-Publication Data is available

...ates of America LAK 0918
...-3 (hardcover)
    7 6 5 4 3 2 1
...722-6 (paperback)
  9 8 7 6 5 4 3 2 1
...8-0724-0 (ebook)

...ks.com
...olishingusa.com

 little bee books

An imprint of Bonnier Publishing USA
251 Park Avenue South, New York, N\
Copyright © 2018 by Bonnier Publi
All rights reserved, including the
in part in any form.
Little Bee Books is a trademar
associated colophon is a trad
Library of Congress Catalo
upon request.
Printed in the United S
ISBN 978-1-4998-0723
First Edition 10 9
ISBN 978-1-4998-0
First Edition 10 9
ISBN 978-1-4990
littlebeeboo
bonnierpu

ALIEN NEXT DOOR

BASEBALL BLUES

by A. I. Newton
illustrated by Anjan Sarkar

little bee books

TABLE OF CONTENTS

1
THE FIRST CATCH

HARRIS WALKER AND HIS BEST FRIEND Roxy Martinez burst out the front door of Harris's house. They clutched baseball gloves, a bat, and a ball in their hands.

The sun shone brightly. The last bits of snow had melted. The first flowers had started to sprout, and a warm breeze mixed with the last of the chilly air.

"It's finally nice enough outside for the First Catch of the Year!" Harris said as he and Roxy ran to opposite sides of his front lawn.

The First Catch of the Year had been a tradition for Harris and Roxy since they were both old enough to throw a baseball.

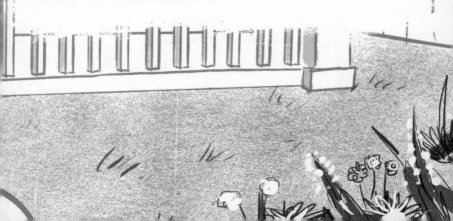

Roxy took a few practice swings with her bat.

"I got this new bat for Christmas," she said. "I can't wait to use it!"

"And I got this new catcher's mitt," Harris said, pounding his fist into the soft leather. "Time to break it in!"

Roxy put down her bat and slipped on her glove. She picked up the baseball and threw it right into Harris's mitt. It landed with a crisp, cracking sound.

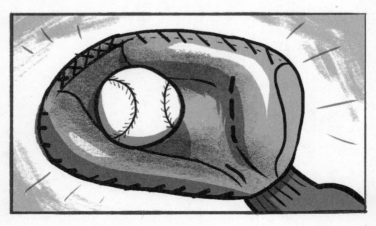

"I can't wait for tryouts!" Harris cried. "I hope I get to play catcher this year."

Harris skipped a ground ball across the lawn. Roxy took two steps to her right, then reached over to field the ball backhanded.

"And I hope I get to play shortstop," Roxy said.

"Keep making plays like that and you'll be on the team for sure!" Harris said.

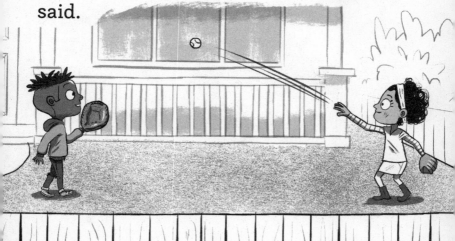

Harris and Roxy planned to try out for the Chargers, the local youth baseball team. The Chargers played against other teams from nearby towns.

Roxy tossed the ball high into the air. "Pop-up!" she yelled.

Harris looked up, raising his glove to shield his eyes from the sun. The ball started to come down.

"Hey, what are you guys doing?" asked a voice from near him.

It was Zeke, Harris's new friend and next-door neighbor, who just happened to be an alien from the planet Tragas. Harris knew his secret. Roxy did not.

"Practicing baseball," Harris replied without taking his eyes off the ball. The pop-up landed in his glove with a soft thud.

"Base . . . ball?" Zeke asked.

"You don't have baseball in Tragas?!" Roxy asked.

Harris and Roxy gave Zeke a quick explanation of the sport. They talked about pitching, fielding, hitting, and running the bases.

Zeke smiled. "This sounds a lot like a game I used to play," he said. "It's called Bonkas. Only in Bonkas, the bats are thinner and ten balls are put into play at the same time!"

"Ten balls!" Roxy exclaimed. "Boy, I have got visit Tragas some time."

"Well, it is pretty far away," Zeke said, glancing slyly at Harris.

"Hey, do you want to play catch, too?" Harris asked Zeke.

"I do," he said. "But I don't have a glove."

"No problem," said Harris. He ran into the house and brought out one of his old gloves. "You can use this."

"Play ball!" shouted Harris.

2 ZEKE AT THE BAT

"IT'S PRETTY SIMPLE, ZEKE," Harris said. "I'll hold up my glove. You try to throw the ball into it."

Zeke stood across the yard from Harris. He threw the ball. It sailed over Harris's head and landed in a neighbor's yard.

"Good try!" Roxy said, trotting over to the ball. "Now try catching."

She tossed the ball softly over to Zeke. He stuck his glove out too late and the ball bounced past him. He ran after it and picked it up.

"Now throw it to me," said Roxy holding up her glove.

Zeke unleashed another throw. This one landed across the street. "I don't know if I can do this," he said sadly.

"All it takes is practice," Harris said. "Let's keep trying."

Zeke's next few throws went onto the roof of a house, bounced off a tree, and splashed into a neighbor's swimming pool.

"Practice, huh?" Zeke said, fishing the wet ball out of the pool.

"Practice," Harris replied, smiling.

They walked back over to the yard. Zeke took a deep breath, reared back, and fired the ball right into Harris's mitt.

"That's it!" Roxy cried. "Now you're getting it!"

Zeke's next throw flew perfectly into Roxy's glove.

"You see?" she said. "You're picking this up really fast!"

But Harris wasn't so sure. Zeke may be an alien, but no one could improve that fast. *Zeke might be using his powers to control the movement of the ball,* he thought. *In a game, something like that would be cheating.*

"Let's try batting next," Harris said, hoping he was wrong about Zeke using his powers. He crouched down into a catcher's position.

Zeke picked up Roxy's new bat and took a couple of practice swings. Then Roxy threw a pitch. Zeke swung early and didn't come close to hitting the ball. It landed in Harris's mitt.

"Follow the ball in, Zeke," Roxy said. "Then time your swing."

Roxy threw another pitch. This time Zeke swung too late.

Harris could see the frustration on Zeke's face.

Zeke swung at Roxy's next pitch and smacked it high into the air. It flew over the roof and into the next yard.

"Wow!" Roxy cried. "Nice one. I want to see where that landed!" She ran off in search of the ball.

"Hey, I know what you're doing, Zeke," Harris said when the two boys were alone. "You're using your powers, aren't you?"

"What's wrong with that?" Zeke asked.

"It's a shortcut and it's cheating," Harris said. "It's not fair to the other players. You need to improve your skills through practice."

"I don't understand," Zeke said. "But I'll try."

Roxy returned with the ball. "You must have hit that 200 feet!" she said.

"Let's keep practicing," said Harris, glancing over at Zeke.

"Yes, practice," said Zeke.

3 TRYOUTS

ON THE DAY OF THE TRYOUTS,
Harris, Roxy, and Zeke arrived at the
field, gloves in hand.

"Harris wants to play catcher and
I want to play shortstop," Roxy said.
"Have you decided on a position,
Zeke?"

"Since we first played, I've been watching a lot of baseball on TV," Zeke said. "I would like to be a pitcher."

"Great!" said Harris. "I hope we all make the team."

Roxy trotted out to short. Zeke stood out on the pitcher's mound. And Harris crouched behind home plate, ready to catch Zeke's pitches.

The first batter stepped into the batter's box. She raised the bat above her shoulders and stared out at Zeke. Behind the plate, Harris held up his glove.

Zeke threw his first pitch. It sailed over the batter's head and crashed into the wooden backstop. ·

"Just focus on my glove, Zeke," Harris shouted.

Zeke's next pitch bounced in the dirt in front of home plate. Harris slid to his right and made a great play to grab the ball before it went past him.

Harris looked out and saw the frustration on Zeke's face. "It's okay, you'll get the next one over, Zeke," he shouted, pounding his mitt a few times with his fist.

Zeke stared at Harris, then threw his next pitch—a big curveball that started way outside, then swept in a huge arc back over the plate. Everyone gasped. It was a perfect pitch!

Zeke's pitch after that did the same thing, but curved in the opposite direction this time. Then he threw a speeding bullet of a fastball that was also a perfect strike.

Harris sighed beneath his catcher's mask. *He's using his powers again*, he thought. *He has to be.*

The next batter hit a ground ball to shortstop. Roxy scooped up the ball and made a perfect throw to first base to get the runner out.

Now at bat, Harris smacked a solid hit to left field. Roxy hit a screamer to right field.

Then Zeke's turn at bat came. He stepped in to bat left-handed. Zeke swung wildly and missed the first two pitches. "Isn't he a righty?" a kid asked. *That's strange*, Harris thought. The pitcher laughed, and Zeke looked embarrassed.

"Remember, Zeke, keep your eye on the ball all the way in!" Harris shouted.

Zeke stared out at the pitcher and gripped the bat tightly. On the next pitch, he used his powers to bring the ball right to the bat.

CRACK!

Zeke's swing sent the ball flying high and deep. It sailed over the outfield fence for the only home run of the day.

"Wow! Way to hit, Zeke!" Roxy shouted.

Everyone on the field cheered as Zeke rounded the bases and crossed home plate.

Everyone except Harris.

The tryout ended and the coach read out the names of the players who had made the team. Harris, Roxy, and Zeke all made it.

"All right! We're going to be on the team together!" Roxy shouted, patting Harris and Zeke on the back.

As the three walked off the field, Harris whispered to Zeke, "We have to talk!"

4 CHEATER?

"I KNOW WHAT YOU DID BACK THERE," Harris said softly when he and Zeke were away from Roxy and the other players.

"It's not a big deal, Harris," Zeke replied. "I'm just using my natural abilities like everyone else."

"But you're *not* like everyone else," Harris said. "That's the point. Using your powers means that you're not learning how to play the game correctly or improve your skills like everyone else."

Zeke looked away.

Harris continued. "Besides, don't you think that using your powers in front of so many people is risky? Aren't you worried that someone might discover your secret? And you took a spot away from someone who deserved it. Promise me you won't use them anymore for baseball."

Harris could tell from the expression on Zeke's face that he hadn't really considered this. "Okay, I promise," Zeke said quietly and walked away.

Over the next few days, Zeke hardly said a word to Harris. For the first time since they became friends, Harris felt a strain in their friendship.

One afternoon after school, Harris decided to talk to Roxy.

"I'm worried about Zeke," he said as they tossed ground balls to each other.

"What do you mean?" she asked, snagging the ball with her glove. "He's been playing well at practice, and everyone on the team seems to really like him."

"I think he may be cheating," Harris said, realizing that he was walking a fine line between helping his friend and guarding Zeke's secret.

"Cheating?!" Roxy said, throwing the ball back to Harris. "Why do you think he's cheating?"

"Um, I'm not sure," Harris said. "But how can someone who never played baseball before suddenly be so good?"

Roxy shook her head. "That doesn't mean he's cheating, Harris. He did say he played a similar game in Tragas, Bonkers or something, so it's probably just that. I think you're a little jealous," she said. "But, now that you mention it, it's pretty amazing that Zeke seems to only throw strikes when he's pitching and hit the ball farther than everyone else—batting both left- and right-handed!"

"That's what I mean," Harris said, tossing the ball high into the air.

"Yeah, it is kind of hard to explain," Roxy said catching the pop-up.

It sure is! Harris thought. *That is, without telling you that Zeke is an alien!*

5 PLAY BALL!

THE DAY OF THE FIRST GAME for the Chargers arrived. Harris, Roxy, and Zeke took the field with their teammates.

The Chargers were playing the Scrappers. Their first batter stepped up to the plate.

"All right, Zeke, here we go!" Harris shouted.

Zeke threw his first pitch. It was way outside. Harris reached out and made a nice catch. The next three pitches also missed by a lot. The batter trotted down to first base with a walk.

"Remember, just focus on my glove!" Harris yelled out to Zeke. "That's your target. Let's go!"

But Zeke had no better luck with the next two batters. He walked each of them on four pitches. The bases were now loaded with nobody out.

Harris called time-out and ran over to Zeke.

"I'm doing what you asked," Zeke said. "I'm playing without using my powers, and look what's happening."

"You're getting a lot better with every pitch, so just try to relax," said Harris. "You'll get the next batter!"

Zeke's next pitch almost flew over Harris's head. He had to stand up and jump to catch it.

Zeke turned his back to the plate. When he turned back around, Harris saw a serious, determined look on his face.

Harris put down one finger, the signal for Zeke to throw a fastball. Zeke nodded, then fired a blazing pitch right over the plate. The batter swung late and missed. The ball slammed into Harris's glove with a thunderous crack for everyone to hear.

"Strike one!" the umpire cried.

The home crowd cheered.

"Come on, Zeke!" shouted Harris's dad from the bleachers.

But Harris was suspicious. *How could Zeke find his control so quickly?* he wondered. *And how did he throw it so fast?*

Harris signaled for the same pitch to see if Zeke could do it twice in a row. He did. Right in the same spot.

"Strike two!" the umpire yelled.

Harris was pretty sure that Zeke was using his powers again. He put down two fingers, signaling for a curveball. *Zeke hasn't been able to throw a curveball yet without cheating. Let's see what he does here*, Harris thought.

Zeke threw a perfect curveball. It looked like it was going to hit the batter—she leaned away from the pitch—but then the ball curved back over the plate.

"Strike three. Yer out!" called the umpire.

Harris was now certain that Zeke using his powers.

"Way to go, Zeke!" Roxy shouted from shortstop.

Mixing fastballs in with curveballs, Zeke easily struck out the next two batters and didn't allow a run to score. As the Chargers headed for the dugout, he headed for the bench with a smile on his face.

Once Zeke sat down and took off his glove, Harris pulled him aside. "You promised," he whispered.

"I'm playing to the best of my ability," Zeke said, looking away. "That's what I'm doing. Nobody else seems to mind."

Roxy walked past Zeke. "Nice job pitching!" she said. "You're up to bat now. Get a hit!"

"See?" Zeke said to Harris, standing up and grabbing a bat.

"Could you please try to hit without using your powers?" Harris asked. "Just try."

Zeke said nothing and strode quietly to the plate.

SUPERSTAR!

ZEKE STEPPED INTO THE BATTER'S BOX.
He glanced over at Harris and nodded,
tight-lipped. He turned and stared at
the pitcher.

Harris took this as a sign that Zeke
had decided not to use his powers.
He watched anxiously as the pitcher
threw her first pitch.

Zeke swung wildly. He didn't even coming close to hitting the ball. The same thing happened on the next pitch, and the one afterward. Three swings, three strikes. Zeke was out.

Harris was up next. As he walked to the plate, he passed Zeke heading back to the bench with his head down.

"Good try, Zeke," Harris said. "Don't worry, you'll get a hit next time."

Zeke said nothing and sat down.

Harris lined the first pitch he saw into left field. After him, the Chargers got a bunch of hits. By the time the inning ended, they had scored three runs.

Back out on the mound, Zeke continued to play without using his powers. His pitching was slowly getting better, but the Scrappers still managed to score three runs to tie up the game.

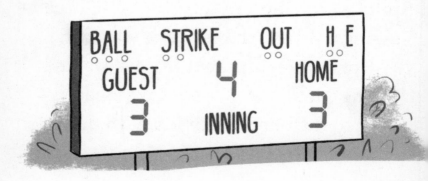

"You're doing good out there, Zeke," Harris said as the two friends sat on the bench.

"But they tied the game," Zeke pointed out.

"It doesn't matter," said Harris. "Your pitching is getting better each inning." And then, lowering his voice, he added: "without any 'extra help.'"

It was Zeke's turn at bat again. And again he swung and missed at three pitches in a row.

Zeke headed back out to the mound. Harris could see the frustration mounting on his face.

"Forget about striking out, Zeke," Harris shouted as he took his position behind the plate. "Let's just get these next three guys out."

Zeke pitched well, but the Scrappers scored a run to take a 4–3 lead heading into the bottom of the final inning.

The first two batters for the Chargers made two quick outs. With nobody on base, Roxy came up to bat.

"C'mon now! Keep it alive, Roxy!" Harris shouted.

Roxy hit the first pitch to right field for a single.

"Yeah!" cried Harris.

Zeke was up next. The game was on the line.

"Just focus, Zeke," Harris said. "You can do it!" Harris was worried that Zeke might use his powers again.

Zeke stepped into the batter's box.

"Do your best, Zeke!" Roxy shouted as she took her lead off first base.

My best, Zeke thought. *Yes, I will do my best.*

The pitcher threw a pitch. Using his powers, Zeke directed the ball right toward his bat. He swung and smacked the ball deep to left field. The ball sailed over the fence for a two-run home run. Zeke had won the game for his team!

All the Chargers rushed onto the
field. They waited as Zeke rounded the
bases. Then the whole team jumped
up and down in a big pile at home
plate with Zeke in the middle.

Everyone except Harris.

"I knew you could do it, Zeke!" Roxy shouted. "You're a superstar!"

I can't join the celebration, Harris thought, *not when Zeke's a cheater!*

THE CROWD OF HAPPY PLAYERS headed off the field. That's when Roxy noticed that Harris wasn't celebrating with the rest of the team.

"Are you really so jealous of Zeke that you can't even be happy for him?" she asked, walking over to Harris. "I'm surprised at you, Harris. I really am."

Harris looked away. He didn't know what to say.

I obviously can't tell Roxy the truth, he thought. *I promised to keep Zeke's secret, even if it costs me his friendship. And I can't celebrate Zeke's cheating and make it seem like I think it's okay for him to use his powers.*

He remained silent.

Roxy rolled her eyes, and stormed off with saying anything else.

Harris met up with his parents in the bleachers.

"What a great win for the Chargers!" his mom said excitedly. "You played so well! And we're so happy for Zeke. He's fitting in and everyone on the team seems to really like him."

"He did good, yeah," Harris said, as they all walked to his parents' car.

"You don't seem all that happy about the game," his dad said.

"No, I'm happy," Harris said. "I'm glad our team won the game and I'm glad Zeke did okay."

"Honey, are you sure you're okay?" his mom asked.

"I'm fine, Mom," Harris said.

I can't talk to anyone about what's really bothering me, he thought. *Anyone, that is, except Zeke!*

After dinner that evening, Harris decided to try to talk to Zeke. He went next door to his house.

"Hello, Harris," said Zeke's father, Xad, answering the door.

"It is nice to see you," said Zeke's mother, Quar. "We are very glad that you have taught Zeke all about bases and balls."

"Yes, he likes this game very much," added Xad.

Harris smiled and nodded, then walked over to his friend. He found Zeke, fingertips on the sides of his head, mind-projecting his homework onto a big screen that hovered above a desk.

"Are you here to tell me to stop using my powers again?" Zeke asked, turning away from the screen.

"I'm here because you're my friend," Harris replied. "And I still think you're not playing fair."

"I'm confused," Zeke said. "My understanding of cheating, as people on Earth use the term, is breaking the rules. I didn't break any rules."

"Well, you're not actually breaking a rule, because there is no rule about aliens using their powers. How could there be?" Harris asked.

"You have never had a problem with me using my powers before when I was careful—like when I saved the camper who fell out of a tree at Beaver Scouts camp. Or when I used my powers to avoid getting hit by a sack of flour at the costume contest. Why is this any different?" Zeke asked.

"I'm not sure," Harris said. "I just know that it is."

"I'll be very careful, Harris. No one will find out," Zeke said.

Harris headed home, frustrated and worried more about his friendship with Zeke than about Zeke using his powers.

Over the next few games, Zeke continued to use his powers. He pitched great and got hit after hit. The Chargers kept winning. He quickly became the most popular player on the team. He teammates even nicknamed him "Superstar."

Everyone was thrilled. Everyone except Harris.

I've never been so miserable about my team winning games, Harris thought. *And I don't know what to do about it!*

8
TAKE ME OUT . . .

HARRIS CONTINUED TO WORRY about the future of their friendship.

One afternoon, on the ride home following another Chargers victory, Harris's parents surprised him.

"How would you like to go to see the Newtown Knights?" his mom said, holding up a handful of tickets.

The Newtown Knights were the local professional minor-league team. Many players from the Knights went on to play in the major leagues. Their stadium was just a few miles from where Harris lived.

"Wow!" Harris said, smiling for the first time in days. "That's so cool!"

"We've loved taking you to see the Knights ever since you were little," his mom said.

"That's where I learned to love baseball!" Harris replied, feeling his mood lifting for the first time in a while.

"And we got enough tickets for Roxy and Zeke to come, too!" his dad added.

Harris's mood sank again. He felt nervous. He really hadn't spent much time with Zeke lately, apart from on the field.

"Great," he said half-heartedly.

About a week later, Harris, Roxy, and Zeke piled into the backseat of Harris's parents' car. His mom and dad rode up front.

"I can't wait to see Dylan Williams," Roxy said. "He's my favorite player."

"Why do you like Dylan Williams so much?" Zeke asked.

"Well, he has the most home runs in the league," Harris jumped in. "He steals lots of bases, and he's a great shortstop. That's why Roxy likes him, since she plays shortstop, too."

"That's true," Roxy added. "But I also like him because he's not a cheater."

Zeke's eyes opened wide. He looked past Roxy, who sat between the two boys, right at Harris. *Could he have said something to Roxy?* Zeke wondered.

Harris's shocked expression told Zeke that he hadn't said anything to Roxy. No matter how upset Harris may have been, he would never betray Zeke's trust by revealing his secret.

"What do you mean by that?" Zeke asked Roxy.

"A few players around the league were caught cheating," Roxy explained. "Some stole the pitching signs from the other team so the batter knew what pitch was coming. Some pitchers were caught throwing spitballs, which is illegal. And some even took steroids."

"Steroids?" Zeke asked.

"It's something the league banned that makes players unfairly strong, no matter how hard the other players exercise and practice."

Harris saw Zeke's expression change. He could see him thinking deeply about what Roxy just said.

They arrived at the stadium and entered the ballpark. The sight of the green field that greeted fans as they walked into the baseball stadium brought smiles to Harris's and Roxy's faces.

Even Zeke, seeing a professional baseball stadium for the first time, was moved by the sight—the lights shining brightly on the field, the buzz of the crowd, and the smells of hot dogs, pretzels, and peanuts.

"Snack time!" said Harris.

"Price's Pretzels!" Roxy shouted.

"Price's Pretzels?" asked Zeke.

"It's a ballpark tradition," explained Roxy. "Come on. We'll show you."

The three friends hurried to the concession stand. They each bought a huge pretzel.

"I have never had a pretzel before," said Zeke.

Harris covered his pretzel with mustard. Roxy smothered hers with cheese instead.

"It's best with mustard," said Harris.

"No way!" said Roxy. "It's *much* better with cheese!"

Zeke stared at his pretzel, then he looked at the container of mustard and the tub of cheese. He squeezed mustard all over his pretzel, then dumped half the tub of cheese on top of that and took a bite.

"Mmm, I like pretzels," he said with his mouth full.

Roxy and Harris laughed and they all headed to their seats.

The Knights took the field. Roxy jumped to her feet and cheered as Dylan Williams trotted out to his position.

"PLAY BALL!" shouted Harris's dad.

9

DYLAN IN ACTION

THE FIRST BATTER HIT A BALL sharply on the ground toward shortstop. Dylan Williams dashed to his left, dove toward second base, and stuck out his glove. He snagged the ball, then popped back up to his feet. He turned and fired the ball to first base in time for the out.

"Yeah, Dylan!" shouted Roxy. "You're the best!"

In the bottom of the inning, Dylan lined a ball that dropped in for a hit.

"Watch him now," Roxy said to Zeke. "He's going to try to steal second."

The next batter stepped up to the plate. Dylan took a few steps off of first. The moment the pitcher started to throw the pitch, Dylan took off for second base.

"There he goes!" Harris shouted.

The catcher threw the ball to the second baseman. Dylan slid into the base.

"Safe!" the umpire shouted.

The crowd roared.

"He did it!" Roxy cried. "He really is the best!"

"I read that Dylan practices stealing more than a hundred times a day, every day," Harris's dad said.

The next player singled and Dylan scored from second base.

Zeke smiled and looked around at the cheering crowd. "This is really fun," he said.

The Knights won the game and Dylan had an all-around great day: hitting, fielding, and stealing bases.

"I have a surprise for you guys," Harris's dad said. "How would you kids like to meet Dylan Williams?"

"Really?!" Roxy asked excitedly.

"Really," said Harris's dad. "One of my business associates is friendly with the owner of the Knights. He set it up so we can meet Dylan. Come on!"

"I can't believe I'm going to meet Dylan Williams!" Roxy said as the group made their way down to the team office.

"Not bad for your first game, huh, Zeke?" Harris said.

Zeke smiled and nodded.

They arrived at the team office where Dylan Williams was waiting. He was still wearing his dirty uniform.

"Nice to meet you kids," Dylan said, shaking each of their hands.

"We all play together on our local youth league team, the Chargers," Harris said.

"That's great, what positions do you play?" Dylan asked.

"I'm a catcher," Harris said. "Zeke is our pitcher."

"And I'm the shortstop, like you!" Roxy said nervously.

Dylan gave a friendly laugh. "You certainly carry yourself like a shortstop!"

Roxy smiled and blushed.

"So, how's your team doing?" Dylan asked.

"We're having a pretty good season," Harris said. "We have a big game coming up against our rivals, the Ramblers, next week."

"Do you have any advice for young players?" Roxy asked. Harris expected Dylan to give her a few fielding or hitting or maybe baserunning tips.

"The best advice I can give you is to stay true to the sport. Never take shortcuts to win. Practice your skills and do the best you can and you'll be a winner no matter what the score is."

Harris and Zeke looked at each other in surprise.

"Thanks so much, Dylan," said Roxy, beaming.

Dylan held up his hand and gave each of them a high five and an autographed baseball.

On the way to the car, Zeke pulled Harris aside.

"I'm sorry," Zeke said. "I've been thinking about what Dylan said. I realize that even though using my powers is natural to me, it does give me an unfair advantage. I can see why it was cheating. And you're right, I need to be more careful with using my powers."

"You're going to be a good ballplayer . . . just by working hard," Harris said.

"I will work on my skills," Zeke said. "But I'm nervous about our big game."

"Only one thing to do," Harris said. "Let's go practice!"

10 ZEKE, A WINNER

FOR EACH OF THE NEXT FEW DAYS, Harris and Zeke practiced for hours. Zeke was now throwing more strikes. And when hitting, Zeke learned to be patient and time his swings.

Harris threw a pitch, and Zeke swung and missed. On the very next pitch however, he hit the ball hard. It flew over Harris's head.

"You're getting better!" Harris said.

"Practice, practice, practice!" Zeke said, smiling.

The day of the big game against the Ramblers finally came. Zeke pitched well. But without using his powers, he gave up three runs. At the plate, he struck out his first time up, but he did manage to hit a few hard foul balls that just missed landing in the field.

In the bottom of the final inning, the Chargers started to rally back. With two outs and a runner on second, Roxy came to bat. She smacked the ball to right field, which scored the Chargers' first run.

"Nice hit, Roxy!" Zeke shouted from the bench.

Harris came up next. He also put the ball in play, scoring Roxy. The Chargers were now trailing 3–2. With Harris on second, they were just one hit away from tying the game.

Zeke came up to bat.

"Come on, Zeke! You got this!" Roxy shouted from the bench.

"Remember what we practiced!" Harris yelled from second base.

Zeke nodded, then stepped in to face the pitcher.

Zeke swung and missed at the first pitch. When the next one came, he drew back the bat, but swung and missed again.

The Chargers were now one strike away from losing.

Zeke looked out at Harris, who gave him a thumbs-up sign. Then he turned to face the pitcher.

Zeke swung at the next pitch.

BOOM!

He hit the ball hard and Harris started running as fast as he could. But the centerfielder tracked down the ball and caught it, so Zeke was out. The ball game was over and the Chargers had lost.

Everyone on the team was disappointed—everyone except Zeke, who trotted back to the bench with a huge smile on his face.

"What are *you* so happy about?" asked one dejected teammate.

"I hit the ball in play!" Zeke said. "And I did it all on my own!"

The teammate looked at him strangely, then walked away.

Harris patted Zeke on the back. He was happy, too.

"Good job," said the coach. "Now, who's ready for a pizza party!"

"When can we practice next?" Zeke asked Harris, who was thrilled that Zeke wanted to keep improving his baseball skills and that they were good friends again.

Harris laughed. "Right after we get some pizza!"

Read on for a sneak peek at the sixth
book in the Alien Next Door series!

THE ALIEN NEXT DOOR

THE MYSTERY VALENTINE

Zeke

6

BY A. I. NEWTON
ILLUSTRATED BY ANJAN SARKAR

ZEKE WALKED INTO JEFFERSON Elementary School. Since his arrival on Earth from the planet Tragas a few months ago, he had started to feel more and more comfortable with Earth customs with each new day. At first, everything on this new planet seemed strange to him. Now, even something that was scary at first, like walking into school, was no big deal.

Except for today.

When Zeke entered the building this February morning, he was shocked by what he saw. The walls were covered with bright red and shiny paper hearts. Curly pink ribbons dangled from the ceiling.

Zeke saw pictures of babies with wings soaring through the sky shooting arrows.

I haven't met any human babies yet, Zeke thought. *Do they really have wings?*

Signs hung everywhere saying: "Be My Valentine!", "I ♥ you!", "It's *heart* not to love you!", "Be my pal-intine!"

Zeke was confused. Normally, the school hallways were filled with posters and signs about school plays, sports competitions against other schools, or class projects. But this? This seemed unusual, even for humans.

Zeke stopped a boy who was hurrying to his first class.

"Um, excuse me, but why is all this stuff up on the walls?" he asked.

The boy shook his head, rolled his eyes, and kept walking. Looking back over his shoulder he said, "What planet are you from, man?"

"Trag—" Zeke started to answer automatically, but caught himself in time. No one but his best friend Harris Walker knew that Zeke was really an alien.

Then the boy stopped and added, "Valentine's Day is next week. What else would it be?"

"I . . . don't . . . know?" Zeke replied as the boy disappeared down the hall. "And what's Valentine's Day?"

At lunchtime, Zeke sat with Harris as he usually did. He was eager to figure out what all these strange decorations were about.

"I have a question," Zeke said. "What is Valentine's Day?"

"Ah, I guess you don't have this holiday on Tragas," Harris said, being sure to keep his voice low to protect his friend's secret.

"No, we don't," Zeke admitted.

"Valentine's Day is a holiday when you let the people that you like know that you care about them," Harris explained. "You can give them a card, or candy, a gift, or something shaped like a heart."

"Now I'm even more confused," said Zeke. "What does the organ that pumps blood through the body have to do with liking someone?"

Harris smiled. "It's just a symbol. On Earth, the heart is the place where you feel an emotion, like love. Don't you have any similar holiday like that on Tragas?"

"Well, we have Hole-tania Day," said Zeke. "That's when each being on Tragas digs a hole and fills it with pieces of furniture they no longer want. Then they invite everyone they love over to see it."

"Um . . . okay," said Harris, a little confused now himself. "Don't worry, Zeke. It's one of those things that might be easier to just experience than to explain. You'll get the hang of Valentine's Day!"

Journey to some magical places, rock out, and find your inner superhero with these other chapter book series from **Little Bee Books!**

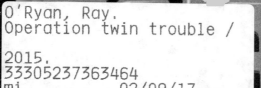

ZACK

OPERATION TWIN TROUBLE

By Ray O'Ryan

Illustrated by Jason Kraft

LITTLE SIMON
New York   London   Toronto   Sydney   New Delhi

LITTLE SIMON
An imprint of Simon & Schuster Children's Publishing Division
1230 Avenue of the Americas, New York, New York 10020
First Little Simon hardcover edition September 2015
Copyright © 2015 by Simon & Schuster, Inc.
Also available in a Little Simon paperback edition.
All rights reserved, including the right of reproduction in whole or in part in any form.
LITTLE SIMON is a registered trademark of Simon & Schuster, Inc., and associated colophon is a trademark of Simon & Schuster, Inc.
For information about special discounts for bulk purchases, please contact Simon & Schuster Special Sales at 1-866-506-1949 or business@simonandschuster.com.
The Simon & Schuster Speakers Bureau can bring authors to your live event. For more information or to book an event contact the Simon & Schuster Speakers Bureau at 1-866-248-3049 or visit our website at www.simonspeakers.com.
Designed by Nicholas Sciacca
Manufactured in the United States of America 0815 FFG
1 2 3 4 5 6 7 8 9 10
Library of Congress Cataloging-in-Publication Data
O'Ryan, Ray.
Operation twin trouble / by Ray O'Ryan ; illustrated by Jason Kraft. —
First Little Simon paperback edition.
pages cm. — (Galaxy Zack ; #12)
Summary: "Zack's twin sisters are best friends, but when the two get into an argument while visiting another planet, Zack finds himself stuck in the middle of a tricky twin situation"— Provided by publisher.
ISBN 978-1-4814-4400-2 (hc) — ISBN 978-1-4814-4399-9 (pbk) —
ISBN 978-1-4814-4401-9 (eBook)
[1. Science fiction. 2. Twins—Fiction. 3. Sisters—Fiction.
4. Brothers and sisters—Fiction. 5. Friendship—Fiction.
6. Human-alien encounters—Fiction.]
I. Kraft, Jason, illustrator. II. Title.
PZ7.O7843Op 2015
[Fic]—dc23
2015006939

CONTENTS

Chapter 1
Game Time!

Zack Nelson stood in the living room of his house on the planet Nebulon. He stared at his friend Drake Taylor.

Zack's parents, Shelly and Otto, sat on their floating shimmer-couch. Zack's twin sisters, Charlotte and Cathy, sat nearby on the floor.

It was family game night at the Nelson house. Three teams were playing Space Charades. Zack and Drake were one team. Charlotte and Cathy were another. And their parents were the third team.

"Ready . . ."

". . . Set . . ."

". . . Go!" the girls shouted together.

A hologram of a digital timer appeared in the air. It was projected by Ira, the Nelson's Indoor Robotic Assistant. The timer started counting off the seconds.

Zack pinned his arms at his sides. He began to jump up and down.

"Jump!" guessed Drake.

Zack shook his head.

"Fly! Leap! High! Ceiling!"

Zack kept shaking his head.

"Bounce!" Drake shouted.

Zack stopped jumping and cupped his hand behind his ear.

"Sounds like bounce?"

Next, Zack held his hands together over his head.

4

"Circle?" guessed Drake. "Zero? . . .
The letter O?"

Zack touched his nose, the sign that
Drake was correct.

"Bounce-O-what?"

Zack pretended he had a shovel
in his hands and was digging in the
ground.

"Dig? Shovel?"

Zack shook his head. He pretended
to throw something into the imaginary
hole he had dug. Then he went back to
his shoveling.

"Bury!" shouted Drake.

Again, Zack touched his nose.

"Bounce-O-Bury," Drake said. He thought for moment.

"Boingoberry!" he shouted.

"That's it!" yelled Zack. He gave Drake a high five.

7

Boingoberries grew all over Venus. They were used to make Zack's favorite shake and syrup.

Drake looked at the timer hologram. "One minute and thirty seconds," he announced. "Pretty good."

"Okay, girls. Your turn," Zack said, taking a seat in his invisible energy chair. He appeared to be sitting on thin air.

8

The girls stood up. They both had flaming red hair. Charlotte kept hers in a ponytail. She also wore a scarf around her neck. Cathy wore her hair in two braided pigtails. This was the only way most people could tell them apart.

"Ready, set, go!" Zack shouted.

Charlotte stuck out her left hand. She then pretended to strum a guitar with her right hand.

"TBD!" Cathy shouted.

"That's it!" Charlotte said. She glanced up at the timer and cheered.

"Five seconds! That's a new record!"
Zack exclaimed from his invisible
chair. "TBD? That's not even a word!"

"Shows what you know. TBD is . . ."

". . . our favorite band. It stands for . . ."

". . . Twin Boys Dancing!"

"No fair," Zack moaned. "How can we compete against two people who do everything together? They even talk like one person."

"I have heard of TBD," said Drake. "In fact, I read that they are playing a concert on their home planet, Mirer."

The girls ran over to their parents.

"Can we . . ."

". . . go . . ."

". . . please?"

"Well," said Mrs. Nelson, "I guess that would be okay."

"Yay!" the girls screeched.

Mr. Nelson scratched his head. "But what about our turn at Space Charades?"

Chapter 2

Journey to Mirer

The space cruiser carrying Zack and his family lifted off from the Creston City Spaceport. They were on their way to the planet Mirer.

The view outside changed from blue sky to black space. Thousands of stars twinkled in the darkness.

"You know, Mom, every time I travel in space, it's just as exciting as the first time," said Zack.

"I know how much you love it, honey," said Mom. "It almost doesn't matter where you are going."

In the seats next to Zack, Charlotte and Cathy could not hold in their excitement.

"I can't believe . . ."

". . . we are going to see . . ."

". . . TBD!" the girls squealed with delight.

"Uh-huh," said Zack. He turned back to his window.

"I take it you're not looking forward to the TBD concert, Captain?" asked Dad.

"No, but I am looking forward to seeing a new planet," Zack said.

"And, when I get home, I can add a 3-D image of Mirer to my holographic planet-collector."

Charlotte and Cathy kept talking about their favorite band.

"I hope they sing . . ."

"... 'Double Trouble.' Oooooh, that's my ..."

"... favorite song! *There are two of us. No, you're not seeing double ...*"

"... *Take us as we are, or there's gonna be trouble!*" the girls sang loudly, then shrieked with excitement.

A short while later an announcement came over the ship's speakers.

"Passengers, we are beginning our landing pattern for Mirer."

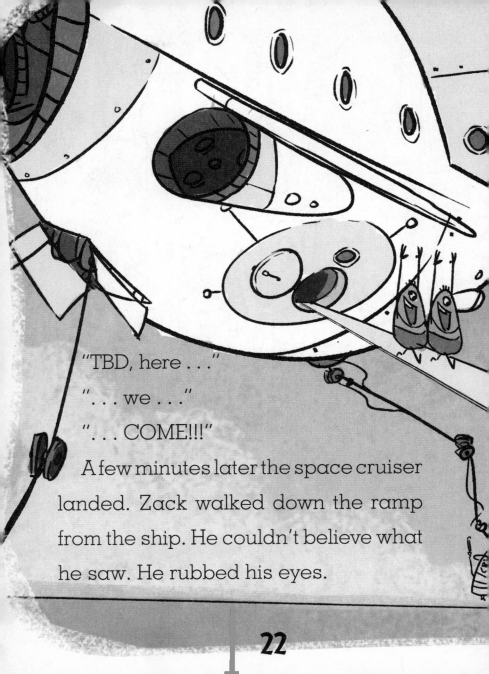

"TBD, here . . ."

". . . we . . ."

". . . COME!!!"

A few minutes later the space cruiser
landed. Zack walked down the ramp
from the ship. He couldn't believe what
he saw. He rubbed his eyes.

"Am I seeing double?" he asked.

"There are two of everything!"

23

Chapter 3

Mirer, Mirer

Zack looked around the Mirer City Spaceport. Mirens looked very much like humans, except that their skin was orange. But Zack had met many aliens since he and his family moved from Earth to Nebulon. Seeing people who looked different was no big deal.

What was a big deal was the fact that every person walking through the spaceport had a twin! Everyone.

"Mommy, can we please have . . ."

". . . four mirlars so we can buy . . ."

". . . a Double-Crunch Duo Bar to share?" said two little boys as they walked past Zack.

"Oh no!" he cried. "Everyone here talks like my sisters!"

The Nelsons reached the flying-car rental area. Dad spoke with the two identical clerks behind the counter.

"We need a car for the five of us," he said.

"Five?" the two clerks said together. They looked right at Zack.

"Your twin couldn't . . ."

". . . make it today? I'm sorry, you must be . . ."

". . . very lonely," the clerks said.

"I don't have a twin," Zack replied.

The two clerks looked at each other in shock.

Zack thought about how Charlotte and Cathy often felt different from everyone else because they were twins. Here in Mirer, he was starting to understand how they felt.

"Here's our car!" said Dad a few seconds later. "Or should I say 'cars'?"

The Nelsons climbed into a car. It had two windshields, two trunks, four headlights, and two sets of seats.

"This looks like two cars glued together!" said Zack.

With everyone in, the Nelsons zoomed out of the spaceport. Zack looked around at Mirer City, the capital of the planet. This was where the TBD concert would take place that evening. They had all day to tour the city.

"There are two of every building!"
Zack said. "Every building has a twin
standing right next to it!"

First, the Nelsons stopped at the
Mirer City Zoo. As Zack walked around,
he saw a whole bunch of animals he
had never heard of.

"Quarnaks," Zack said, reading the first sign. "Four-legged creatures with fur and wings. And there are two of them!"

"Mumbrads," he said, reading the next sign. Two identical huge green beasts stood side by side. "They look like an elephant crossed with a hippo and a rhino!"

33

"I love . . ."

". . . this zoo! There are two . . ."

". . . of everything!" said the girls.

Zack suddenly noticed the sky
getting darker. He looked up and saw
gray clouds moving in front of Mirer's
two suns.

Rain started pouring down. The Nelsons ran for cover in the zoo's snack shack.

"Since we're here," said Dad, rubbing his hands together, "who wants a snack?"

"We do!" Charlotte and Cathy shouted together.

"Me too," said Zack. He glanced at the menu.

"A Double-Dual-Ice-Cream Planet," he said. "I want one of those. Or should I say . . . two of those!"

Zack's snack arrived. His eyes opened wide. The bowl was black, covered in white dots that looked like stars. In the bowl were two huge scoops of ice cream. Bright orange marshmallows orbited around the ice cream "planets" like tiny moons.

Outside, thunder cracked and lightning flashed. Zack looked out the window. Every lightning flash contained two jagged white bolts.

"Even the lightning here comes in pairs!" said Zack. Then he shoved another spoonful of ice cream into his mouth.

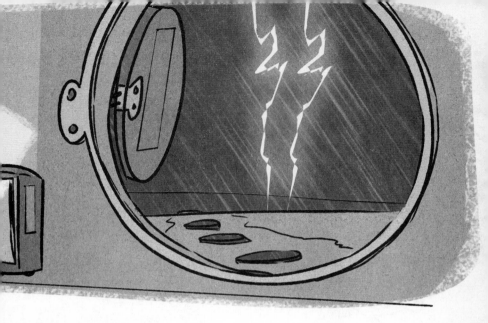

A few minutes later, the rain slowed down. The clouds began to break up, and sunlight poured through. There in the sky, a double rainbow appeared.

"This is the coolest planet . . ."

". . . in the galaxy!"

"Twins rule!" the girls cheered.

Chapter 4
Twin Boys Dancing!

The Nelsons spent the rest of the day touring Mirer City. Zack couldn't get over the fact there were two of everything. Kids in the park played a version of soccer—with two balls at once. Others rode jet-powered hoverboards—one for each foot!

Dinner at the Double Down Diner was twin galactic patties. "At least they have food I like here—even if it is just two patties on two buns," said Zack.

For dessert Zack had a mondo-chocolate layercake—two cakes, four layers each. The twins shared a helping of doubleberry pie. Doubleberries grew throughout Mirer, and always in pairs.

42

After dinner, it was finally time for the concert.

"Twin . . ."

". . . Boys . . ."

". . . Dancing! Here we come!" the girls shouted.

The Nelsons drove to the arena
where the concert was going to take
place. It was called the Dual Dome.

Zack looked up at two round domes
rising from a flat platform. "This place
looks like a big, bald, two-headed
monster," he said.

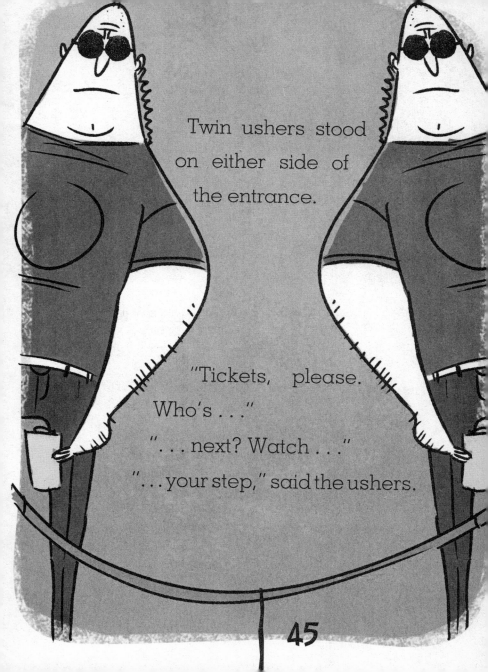

Twin ushers stood
on either side of
the entrance.

"Tickets, please.
Who's . . ."
". . . next? Watch . . ."
". . . your step," said the ushers.

45

A few minutes later, Zack, the twins, and his parents were in their seats. The lights went down and the crowd cheered.

Then a voice boomed from the arena's giant speakers. "Twins of all ages! Please welcome Mirer's own Twin . . . Boys . . . Dancing!"

The Twin Boys burst onto the stage. Of course, they were wearing identical outfits. Tiny rows of colored lights blinked across their shirts. Lasers flashed from their boots. They each grabbed a microphone and launched into their first song: "Double Crush!"

"No matter what you do . . ."

". . . you can count from one to two . . ."

". . . but still it will be true . . ."

". . . I've got a double crush on you!"

Charlotte and Cathy sang along with every word. The also imitated the hand movements that the boys made. Before the song was over, they were

up and dancing. So was every other girl in the place.

Zack's parents bobbed their heads in time with the music. They were glad that the girls were having so much fun.

Zack, on the other hand, was bored out of his mind.

These guys have nothing on Retro Rocket! he thought. Retro Rocket was Zack's favorite band from Earth. He began thinking about intermission, when he could go see what double-size snacks were for sale.

After several songs, a spotlight started moving across the audience.

"Okay, girls . . ."

". . . this is the part of the show . . ."

". . . when one lucky fan gets to dance with us on stage!" the boys shouted.

The crowd went wild.

Cries of "Pick me!" echoed throughout the arena.

Suddenly, the spotlight stopped. It landed right on Charlotte!

"Come up, little lady, and . . ."

". . . dance with . . ."

"Twin . . . Boys . . . Dancing!"

51

Charlotte jumped from her seat and ran toward the stage. Cathy jumped up too, running close behind her sister.

Charlotte reached the stage. One of the Twin Boys leaned down and offered her a hand. Two security guards stepped out right in front of Cathy.

"I'm sorry. Only one guest . . ."
". . . is allowed on the stage," said the security guards.

"But I'm her sister!" Cathy cried. The guards looked back toward the stage. Charlotte was dancing with the Twin Boys.

"It looks like she's doing . . ."

". . . just fine by herself," said the guards.

"Now please go back to your seat."

Cathy was crushed. She had never been jealous of anyone in her life. And now she was jealous of her own sister! She walked slowly back to her family.

Up onstage, Charlotte danced, holding hands with the boys. A huge smile beamed from her face.

"Now this is great, isn't it?" Dad said to Cathy.

Cathy said nothing. She sat with her arms crossed. She wished she was up onstage in Charlotte's place.

Chapter 5
Long Ride Home

Following the concert, the Nelsons boarded the space cruiser for the ride home. Charlotte could not stop talking about her time onstage.

"And then they twirled me around and around," she said excitedly. "And just when I thought I might fall, the

Twin Boys lifted me into the air! And everyone cheered—for me!"

Zack quickly realized two things. First, he was really getting tired of hearing about the concert. And second, he could not remember the last time that he heard one of the twins complete a sentence by herself.

"That's wonderful, honey," said Mom. She smiled at Charlotte, then looked over at Cathy. Cathy stared down at the floor between her feet and frowned. Mom was happy for Charlotte. But she was worried about Cathy, who was obviously feeling left out.

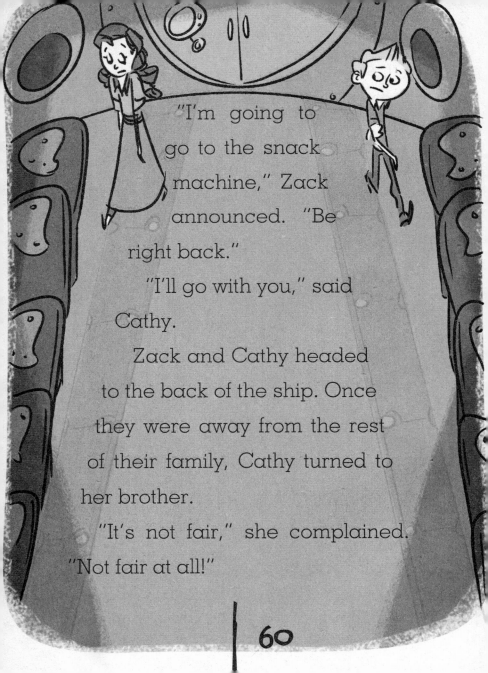

"I'm going to go to the snack machine," Zack announced. "Be right back."

"I'll go with you," said Cathy.

Zack and Cathy headed to the back of the ship. Once they were away from the rest of their family, Cathy turned to her brother.

"It's not fair," she complained. "Not fair at all!"

"What's not fair?" asked Zack.

"Charlotte got to go onstage, but I didn't," she said. "I mean, just because we look alike doesn't mean we are the same person."

"You could have fooled me," said Zack. He couldn't resist giving his sister a hard time.

"Well, we're not!" Cathy shouted. "We are two *different* people!"

Zack could not recall the last time he had a conversation this long with only one of his sisters.

Zack and Cathy arrived at the snack machine. The choices included brick bark, crispy fritters, and nebu-nuts. While they were deciding, a tall girl near the snack machine stood up and pointed at Cathy. "Hey, look, everybody. It's the girl who got to dance with TBD!" she said.

63

Cathy smiled for the first time all day. *Maybe I can get a little bit of the attention,* she thought. *No one will know that it wasn't me up on that stage.*

But just as Cathy opened her mouth, Charlotte stepped up to the snack machine.

"Actually, I was the one dancing with TBD," she said.

Cathy looked super-annoyed. "You couldn't even pretend it was me for one minute?" she asked.

"Well, it wasn't you—it was me!" replied Charlotte.

It was strange to see his sisters argue, but Zack was kind of enjoying this surprising trouble in twinland.

Chapter 6
Shopping Spree

The next morning, Zack hurried downstairs.

"Good morning, Master Just Zack," said Ira. "Would you like your usual breakfast?"

"You bet! Thanks, Ira," said Zack.

"Preparing nebu-cakes," said Ira.

"And don't forget the boingoberry syrup!" said Zack.

A moment later a steaming stack of nebu-cakes slid out of an opening in the kitchen counter. As Zack gobbled up his breakfast, Charlotte came downstairs. Cathy followed a few seconds later.

"Good morning, Charlotte. Good morning, Cathy," said Ira. "Would you

both like your usual bowl of Cosmic Crispies?"

"Sure. Thanks, Ira," said Charlotte. She was still beaming from her time onstage with TBD.

"No," said Cathy. "If she's having that, then I want something else. I'll have nebu-cakes, like Zack."

Charlotte glared at her sister.

"Well, if she's not having our usual

breakfast, I won't either," she said. "I'll have a bowl of Astro-Flakes."

Mom burst into the kitchen.

"Who wants to go to Cisnos for a quick shopping trip?" she asked, smiling.

"I do!" cried Cathy.

"Me too!" said Charlotte.

"Sure," said Zack. "I finally have enough on my allowance card to get that retro remote-control space cruiser!" He raced to get his card.

"Well, hurry up, girls, and finish your breakfast," said Mom. "Then go and brush your teeth."

After speeding through breakfast—Cathy had nebu-cakes and Charlotte had Astro-Flakes—the girls went to get ready.

A few seconds later, Zack and his mom heard a shriek from upstairs. They rushed to see what had happened.

"Look at this!" Charlotte cried. She held up a shredded scrap of clothing. "Luna chewed up my favorite scarf!"

Luna, the Nelson's dog, was still chomping on a piece of the scarf.

"Now no one will be able to tell me apart from Cathy."

"Why don't we get you a new scarf?" Mom suggested.

"If *she* gets something new to wear, *I* want something new to wear too!" said Cathy.

"Of course, honey," said Mom.

Zack rolled his eyes and headed downstairs. After a short space flight, Zack, Mom, and the twins arrived at the Cisnos Mondo-Mall.

Zack had almost forgotten how huge the mall was. Stores spread out in every direction. The mall was ten stories tall.

"I want to go to Celestial Clothes!" Cathy shouted. She pulled on Mom's left arm.

"I want to go to Orbital Outfits!" shouted Charlotte. "I like the clothes there much better." She pulled on Mom's right arm.

"I'll see you guys later," said Zack. He wanted to get as far away from his stressed sisters as possible.

Zack remembered that the Mondo-Mall had Midge—the Mall Interactive Directory Guide Escort. It helped shoppers find whatever they were looking for. It also guided family members back to a meeting point when they were finished shopping.

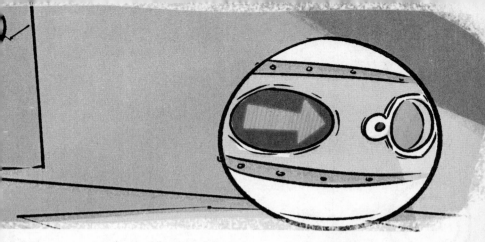

"Midge, where can I find the retro remote-control space cruiser?" asked Zack.

A small round metal ball appeared, floating in the air.

"I am Midge," said a voice coming from a speaker on the flying ball. "I am here to help you. Simply follow your name, Zack."

Zack's name appeared on the floor.

His name started moving.

"Meet you later, Mom!" he said. Then he took off.

Zack worked his way through the mall, heading toward the toy store. He thought about his sisters. He wished that they would start getting along again.

At first, their arguing was kind of funny. After all, they've always been more like one person than two. But now, this was really becoming a problem.

And Zack saw that it really bothered Mom. Maybe *he* could fix the problem!

It was time for: Operation Twin Trouble!

Chapter 7
Operation Twin Trouble

Zack finally arrived at Terrifically Tremendous Toys, the biggest toy store in the Mondo-Mall.

"Wow!" he said, looking around at the cool gadgets. He saw a jet pack, a robot, a holographic car, and so many other incredible toys.

Zack wanted everything. But this store was very expensive. It took him weeks to save up enough for the retro remote-control space cruiser. But it only took a few seconds to find it.

Zack grabbed one of the boxes and headed to the counter to pay.

"Thank you for shopping at our Terrifically Tremendous Toys," said the sales clerk. "As a bonus, everyone who buys a toy today gets a free Cosmic Karen doll."

Maybe this doll can help bring my sisters back together, Zack thought. *Operation Twin Trouble is underway.*

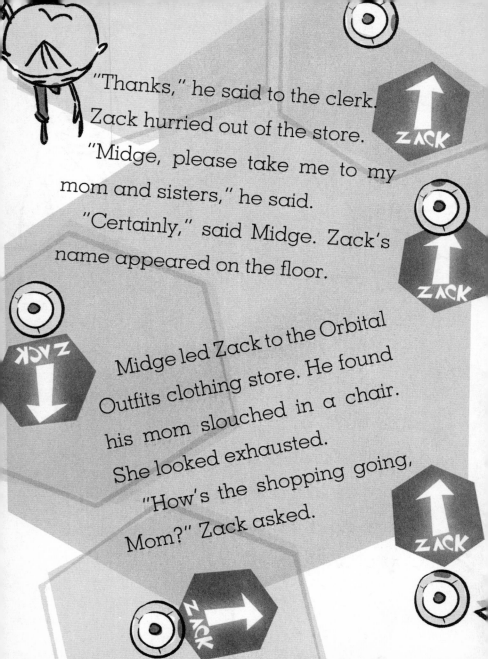

"Thanks," he said to the clerk. Zack hurried out of the store.

"Midge, please take me to my mom and sisters," he said.

"Certainly," said Midge. Zack's name appeared on the floor.

Midge led Zack to the Orbital Outfits clothing store. He found his mom slouched in a chair. She looked exhausted.

"How's the shopping going, Mom?" Zack asked.

Before Mom could answer, Charlotte popped out of a dressing room. Cathy stepped out of the dressing room next-door.

Charlotte was wearing a new scarf and a long skirt with flowers that moved. They looked as if they were blowing in a gentle breeze.

Cathy, on the other hand, wore a pair of jeans covered in what looked like soft fur.

"My skirt is so much cooler than your jeans," said Charlotte.

"No way!" Cathy shouted. "My jeans are as soft as Luna's fur!"

"Girls, really," Mom said. "Can't you both have nice outfits? Why does one have to be better?"

"I think I have a way to make both of
you happy," said Zack. He pulled the
Cosmic Karen doll from his bag. "A
brand-new Cosmic Karen doll!"

Cathy snatched the doll out of Zack's
hands. She gave him a big hug.

"Thanks, Zack," she squealed. "You
are best brother ever!"

Charlotte grabbed the doll and tried to yank it away from Cathy.

"Obviously, Zack got the doll for me, not you!" Charlotte said. She pulled hard. One of Cosmic Karen's arms snapped right off.

"That's enough," said Mom. "You girls need to share."

"I'm tired of sharing everything just because we're twins!" both girls said angrily.

Operation Twin Trouble is off to a shaky start, thought Zack.

Chapter 8
Phase Two

Back at home, Zack decided to work extra hard to help his sisters be friends again. He found Cathy in her room.

"Remember how I used to joke about you and Charlotte finishing each other's sentences?" he asked.

"Yeah," said Cathy.

"Well, now I miss that," said Zack.
"I think it would be great if you two got
along again."

"Why should we?" asked Cathy.

"Well, you are sisters," said Zack.
"You've been together every minute of
your life for eleven years. Doesn't that
count for something?"

"Yeah, it counts for lots of time I wasted," said Cathy.

"But you've always liked to play together," said Zack. "Like, all the dolls you've shared."

"If they are dolls that she liked, I don't want them!" said Cathy.

She went into her closet and pulled out a big box of dolls. She sorted through them, handing some to Zack.

"I don't want this one . . . or this one . . . or, oh, this one was her favorite," said Cathy. "She can have all of these. Just give them to her."

Zack's arms were full of dolls. The pile reached up to his nose. He had to look over it to see where he was going.

Zack stumbled downstairs, bumping into walls. He tried not to drop the stack of dolls. Even Luna had to help him. Charlotte was sorting through piles of clothes in the Nelson's playroom.

"What are those?" Charlotte asked.

"These are dolls that Cathy thought you might like," said Zack. He knew that this was not exactly what Cathy had said. But he hoped that the dolls could bring some peace between the sisters.

Charlotte leaned in close to her brother. "If they were hers, I don't want them!" she said.

Zack took a step back and tripped over a pile of clothes on the floor. He fell back. The dolls scattered all over the room.

"I'm getting rid of all my clothes that are the same as Cathy's," Charlotte said.

She gathered up a big bundle and shoved the clothes into Zack's arms.

"Here, I don't want to wear these anymore," said Charlotte. "Give them to Cathy.

Once again Zack had his arms full with a pile that nearly covered

his eyes. Stumbling back upstairs, he went to Cathy's room.

"What are you holding?" Cathy asked.

"Clothes that Charlotte thought you would like," Zack said. He hoped this plan, which didn't work so well on Charlotte, might work on Cathy.

No such luck.

"I don't want these outfits if they came from her!" shouted Cathy.

She quickly pulled out a shirt from the bottom of the pile in Zack's arms. The whole bundle of clothing tumbled to the floor.

"I don't want any of this stuff," said Cathy.

Zack went to his room. He laid down on his bed. Luna sat beside him.

"I don't know what to do, Luna," he said, scratching her head. "I'm exhausted from going back and forth, trying to patch things up. And nothing I do seems to work. Operation Twin Trouble is a failure!"

Chapter 9
The Longest Dinner

That night at dinner, Zack sat between Charlotte and Cathy. They had always sat next to each other. Since returning from Mirer, they had been sitting apart. And they refused to speak to each other.

"Zack, can you ask my sister to pass the peas?" Cathy said.

"Charlotte, can you pass the peas?" Zack asked.

Charlotte handed the bowl of peas to Zack. He then passed it on to Cathy.

Maybe this might help bring them together, Zack secretly hoped.

"Zack, will you ask my sister to pass the bread?" Charlotte said.

"Cathy, can you pass the bread?"
Zack asked.

"Zack, can you tell my sister that I
haven't taken my piece of bread yet,"
said Cathy.

"Zack, can you tell my sister that she
has had the bread for half the meal,"
said Charlotte. "Tell her she should
learn to share."

"Me? Learn to share?" shouted Cathy. "I'm not the one who got to dance with TBD."

"Girls, I do wish you would try to get along," said Mom. "Just the other day you were working together as a great team when we were playing Space Charades."

Maybe that's it, thought Zack. *Maybe playing a game can bring them back together!*

"Speaking of Space Charades," Zack said, "why don't we play after dinner? I can ask Drake to come by."

"That's a wonderful idea, Zack," said Mom.

"Absolutely," Dad agreed. "Especially since Mom and I didn't get our turn last time!"

"I'll play, as long as Cathy is not on my team," said Charlotte.

"I call dibs on Zack," said Cathy.

"Good. I call dibs on Drake," said Charlotte.

This was not what Zack had in mind. Still, at least the girls would be playing the same game. He grabbed his hyperphone and sent a message to Drake.

Chapter 10

Teamwork

After dinner Drake arrived. He joined the Nelsons in the living room for a game of Space Charades.

Mom and Dad went first.

Mom took her index finger and her middle finger and made a cutting motion.

"Cut? Chop. Snip?"

Mom shook her head, then repeated the motion.

"Scissors!" Dad shouted.

Mom touched her nose. The she started shaking her head.

"Head? Shake? Ummm . . . No!"

Mom touched her nose.

"Scissor-know," said Dad. "Scissor know? Cisnos!" he shouted.

"You got it," said Mom.

Cathy read the floating timer. "Fifty-one seconds," she said. "Our turn."

Cathy and Zack stood up. Zack began.

He pretended to put food into his mouth.

"Eat? Chew? Taste?"

Zack shook his head.

He repeated the
eating gesture, then
pointed at his hand.

"Finger? Food? Fork?
Knife? Spoon?"

Zack touched his nose.

"Spoon . . . spoon something."

Next, Zack opened his mouth and
pressed his finger
on his tongue.

"Mouth . . .
tongue . . . Argh!
I don't know.
You are terrible
at this game."

Zack kept trying. The timer passed two minutes, then three, then four.

Cathy threw her hands up in frustration. "I give up."

"I was going for 'aah' like you say when the doctor looks at your throat," Zack explained. "Spoon-aah."

"What is 'spoon-aah'?"

"Sounds like 'Luna.' I was going for 'Luna.'"

"All you had to do was pretend you were a dog," said Cathy. "I would have gotten it in two seconds."

Charlotte and Drake were next. They didn't do much better.

Drake was trying to act out the word "hyperphone," but all his clues left Charlotte staring at him blankly. In the end Charlotte gave up too.

"I guess Mom and I are the winners," said Dad.

"That's because . . ."

". . . boys are really bad at . . ."

". . . playing Space Charades."
Charlotte and Cathy said.

They looked at each other for a
second. They had not finished each
other's sentences in days.

The girls both smiled.

"Let's play again. This time . . ."

". . . it's the boys . . ."

". . . against the girls!"

"You got it!" said Zack. He was thrilled that the girls were getting along again. And he had never been so excited about losing a game.

GALAXY ZACK

ADVENTURE!

HERE'S A SNEAK PEEK!

Zack Nelson stood in front of his house on the planet Nebulon. He was waiting for the Sprockets Speedybus to pick him up to go to Sprockets Academy.

Suddenly, a silver blur appeared in the distance.

There's the bus, he thought.

An excerpt from *Science Fair Disaster!*

The blur stopped right [ ] Zack. The bus doors opene[ ] climbed on board.

The bus was filled with kids talking and laughing. As Zack headed toward the back, he overheard a bunch of conversations.

"My idea is to build a robot that can play galactic blast with you and transform into a hover car to take you anywhere you want to go," said a boy.

"I am going to build a machine that recycles garbage into clean fuel," said a girl. "Then I am use that fuel for my hyper-ener-verter to power my house."

An excerpt from *Science Fair Disaster!*

dioactive Surge-a-Matron
k atoms even smaller," said another boy as Zack walked past.

Zack spotted his friend Drake Taylor. Drake was busy scribbling on his electro-note-screen with his finger.

Zack sat down next to him.

"What's going on?" asked Zack. "When did everyone at Sprockets Academy become so interested in science?"

Drake looked up. "Ever since this morning when Sprockets was picked to host the Intergalactic Science Fair!" he said excitedly.

An excerpt from *Science Fair Disaster!*